THE PUZZLE CLUB™
CASE OF THE
KIDNAPPED KID

by Dandi Daley Mackall

Based on characters developed for *The Puzzle Club Christmas Mystery*, an original story by Mark Young for Lutheran Hour Ministries

Lutheran Hour
Ministries

SAINT LOUIS

Puzzle Club™ Mysteries
The Puzzle Club Christmas Mystery
The Puzzle Club Mystery of Great Price
The Puzzle Club Case of the Kidnapped Kid
The Puzzle Club Poison-Pen Mystery

Cover illustration by Mike Young Productions

Scripture quotations taken from the HOLY BIBLE, NEW INTERNATIONAL VERSION®. NIV®. Copyright © 1973, 1978, 1984 by International Bible Society. Used by permission of Zondervan Publishing House. All rights reserved.

Copyright © 1998 International Lutheran Laymen's League

™ Trademark of International Lutheran Laymen's League

Published by Concordia Publishing House
3558 S. Jefferson Avenue, St. Louis, MO 63118-3968
Manufactured in the United States of America

1 2 3 4 5 6 7 8 9 10   07 06 05 04 03 02 01 00 99 98

Contents

1

The Threat

"You're out!" Patrick Grimaldi yelled the words an instant before Alex felt the spike in his knee.

Alex winced in pain, but he kept sliding. He stuck out his arm and felt home plate under his fingers.

"Safe!" yelled the umpire behind the plate. "You need to tag him, catcher. He slid past you."

"He's out!" Patrick yelled. He leaned down into Alex's face so close, Alex could smell the cinnamon gum Patrick always chewed.

"I am not out!" Alex said. He started to get up, but his knee hurt when he bent it. He looked down at the hole in his jeans from Patrick's spikes. Blood was clotting around the cut, mixing with the dust from the baseball field.

"Game's over," announced Coach Bryan, coach of Patrick's team. "Alex just scored the winning run."

Alex flopped over on his back. He could hear his teammates cheering in the dugout. He lay across home plate, staring up at Coach Bryan's big belly. The coach put his arm around Patrick's shoulders. Alex reached out and grabbed at Patrick's leg. All he got was a shoelace. He held on.

"Just a minute, Grimaldi," Alex said. "You can't get away with that. I don't care if your dad *is* the sheriff. It's not fair. You spiked me in the knee."

"Get over it, Alex!" said Patrick.

"Don't pay any attention to him, Alex," Korina said, coming to home plate with the rest of the team. "We won the game." Korina had her glove under one arm, her baseball cap pushed back on her head. Korina was one of the reasons the team had made it to the play-offs. Even Alex had to admit that Korina was a great pitcher.

Christopher bent over Alex, blocking the bright sunlight. "You okay, Alex?" Christopher asked. He checked Alex's knee.

Alex still clutched Patrick's shoelace. "No, I'm not okay, thanks to *him*. You should be thrown out of Junior League, Grimaldi! Hey, I'm talking to you."

But Patrick Grimaldi didn't seem to hear Alex or to realize he was still being held prisoner by his shoelace. Patrick's hand shielded his eyes as he stared into the bleachers. His head moved slowly, from side to side, as Coach Bryan mumbled to him.

Christopher straightened up and looked where Patrick was staring. "If you're looking for your dad, Patrick, I saw him on the north field. He was watching your brother's game."

Patrick's brother, Joseph, was Christopher's age, 14. They were the oldest players in the city's Junior League, which was a mixed league for boys and girls. Alex and Patrick were among the youngest players in the league.

Patrick kicked his foot and jerked his shoelace out of Alex's hand. It left a small rope burn on Alex's palm.

"I'm not looking for my dad," Patrick said. "Come on, Coach, let's get out of here."

Christopher and Korina each took an elbow to help Alex up. Alex watched Patrick walk off with Coach Bryan. "Hey, come back here, Grimaldi!" he yelled. "I'm not through with you yet."

"Let him go, Alex," Christopher said. "We won. We're in the finals tomorrow against Joe's team."

"Yeah," said Korina. "As you're so fond of saying, 'Lighten up.' It doesn't matter."

Alex touched his sore knee. "Well, it matters to me. Patrick's always like that. You two don't have to put up with him in school like I do. He thinks he can do anything he wants because his dad's the sheriff." Alex brushed the dirt from his jeans and wished he had a jersey like the one Patrick's team had.

Christopher seemed to read Alex's mind. "You know, Tobias says he might be able to get baseball uniforms for our team next year. Jerseys at least. They'd say *Puzzleworks* on the back." Alex liked that. But he wasn't ready to stop being mad yet.

Suddenly, they heard angry voices. An argument had broken out behind one of the dugouts. Alex, Korina, and Christopher turned toward the voices.

"... deserve a rematch!" Coach Bryan was yelling loud enough to be heard all over the field.

"That's the craziest thing I have ever heard of!" said Coach Miles.

Alex had never heard Coach Miles, their Junior League baseball coach, yell that loud—not even when a player was picking flowers in the outfield. He was a good coach, even though he didn't know much more about baseball than what he read in his *Sports Illustrated* magazines between innings.

"Well, we'll just see about that," barked Coach Bryan. "I'm submitting an official appeal to the Junior League. If they agree, the rematch will be tomorrow. And you can count on it that the league *will* agree."

"They can't do that, can they, Christopher?" Korina asked. "We won fair and square, 6 to 5. They can't make us play it over, can they?"

Christopher shrugged. The argument between the coaches was still going full force.

"Because we don't have fancy uniforms like you do?" Coach Miles asked in a high voice.

"Read the rules, Miles," said Coach Bryan. "Section 4 … uh … 43 …" He leaned down and Patrick whispered something in his ear. "Section 432 of the Junior League rules clearly says *uniformed players*. Maybe this will be a lesson to you. Teach those kids of yours to play by the rules."

"Why you … you …" Poor Coach Miles couldn't get the words out. "You better not do this, Bryan," he said through clenched teeth.

"Oh yeah, *Coach* Miles?" said Coach Bryan. "And just what do you think you're going to do about it?"

Alex held his breath as he watched the two men. Patrick had moved away, leaving the coaches standing alone, nose to nose. Coach Bryan was a good foot taller and 50 pounds heavier than Coach Miles. Alex just hoped the men wouldn't actually fight.

"You don't think I'll do anything about it, do you, Bryan?" asked Coach Miles in a low, steady voice. "Think I'm too much of a wimp, right? Well, I'm not the same little boy you used to bully in elementary school. You can only push a man so far. And you, Bryan, have pushed far enough! You take back your demand for a rematch with my Puzzleworks team or you'll be sorry."

"Are you threatening me, Miles?" Coach Bryan asked, puffing up his already enormous chest.

"Threatening you?" Coach Miles asked in a strange voice Alex had never heard him use before. "No, I'm not *threatening* you. I'm making you a *promise*. If you try for a rematch, I'll make you wish you hadn't."

Despite the hot sun and the sweat beading on his face, Alex felt an icy chill travel down his spine. Somehow he knew this game wasn't over.

2

Alex's Revenge

Alex congratulated his teammates for winning the play-off game. One more game and they would win the city's Junior League championship. The championship game would be played at Victory Field! The town used Victory Field strictly for championship games. No one on his team had ever played a game there.

Alex limped back to Puzzleworks with Christopher and Korina. They wanted to tell Tobias the good news about their victory. Halfway there, Alex's knee stopped stinging, but his heart hadn't stopped stinging. More than ever, he wanted to get even with Patrick Grimaldi.

"... a couple of practices. Maybe one on Victory Field, if we can get up early enough."

Christopher had been talking, but Alex hadn't been listening.

"Alex," Korina scolded, "you haven't heard a word we've said. What are you thinking about?"

Alex didn't want to tell Korina what he was thinking about. He'd been thinking about revenge. And he knew Christopher wouldn't like it either. Revenge wasn't exactly what God's children were supposed to be thinking about. He was pretty sure Jesus had never taken revenge on anybody.

"I was just wondering if we'd have to play a rematch," Alex said. It was *one* of the things he'd been thinking about.

"Could be," Christopher said. "We just barely beat them this time too. And even if we can beat Patrick's team again, it will wear us down before the championship game."

"This is true," Korina said, rubbing her shoulder. She pulled out her magnifying glass and held it to the baseball in her glove. Then she peered through the glass, as if she could see all the answers. "We will need to be in top condition to face Joseph Grimaldi's team in the finals. Now *he's* one great baseball player."

"He ought to be," Christopher said. "Joe and his dad have worked on his game since Joe was in kindergarten. I think he wants to play professional baseball someday."

Light reflected off Tobias' storefront window as Alex, Korina, and Christopher crossed the street in front of Puzzleworks. Even the bricks in the walls looked like puzzle pieces. From outside, the store seemed as cheery and welcoming as Tobias himself. Alex loved going to Puzzleworks.

Alex wanted to be the one to report to Tobias. He threw open the door and ran in first. "Tobias!" he hollered.

"Over here, Alex," called their friend. "Don't slam the door."

Alex peered around the little puzzle shop. The walls were lined with wood puzzles, plastic puzzles, cardboard puzzles. Racks of odd-shaped puzzles and boards lay everywhere.

Tobias stood on a wooden stool, his arms stretched toward the ceiling light fixture. He pressed two last puzzle pieces into the shade of the lamp.

"It's my latest puzzle," Tobias said. "A lamp shade puzzle." Tobias climbed down from the stool and took a deep breath. He ran his fingers through his white hair. "Turn the light on and we'll take a look."

Korina flipped on the light. The shade lit up into dim outlines of puzzles pieces. Alex stared at it until he could make out a kangaroo, two giraffes, and a big wooden boat with other animals. "Noah's ark?" he asked.

"Yes!" Tobias said, sounding pleased.

"Tobias," Alex said, remembering why they'd come to the shop, "we won!"

"Wonderful," Tobias said. "I wish I could have seen the game."

"Well, you may get another chance," Christopher said. "Coach Bryan is demanding a rematch."

Korina and Christopher explained everything to Tobias. Alex had his mind on other things, like Patrick Grimaldi. It was all Patrick's fault, Alex knew. Coach Bryan wouldn't have thought about asking for a rematch if Patrick hadn't been such a lousy sport.

Alex decided it was up to him. He'd have to get even with Patrick and make him call off the rematch. This wasn't the first time Patrick Grimaldi had caused Alex trouble. It was about time Alex did something about it.

"Alex, what do you think?" Tobias called from behind his counter.

"Huh?" Alex asked.

"Tobias says he'll help us come up with some kind of uniform if we have to play a rematch," Christopher said.

"There's not going to be a rematch," Alex said firmly.

"We don't know that, Alex," Christopher said.

"You heard me," Alex said. "No rematch."

Tobias stared at Alex with a strange look on his face.

Korina turned and gave Alex one of her looks too. "Alex has been out of it ever since he got spiked while scoring the winning run today," she said. "I think the sight of his own blood scared him."

"I've seen my own blood lots of times. I was not scared," Alex said. But that was all he needed to seal his plan. Alex would have to get even with Patrick once and for all.

"Tobias," he said. "Please pull the cord."

"B-B-But Alex," Tobias pleaded, stuttering a little, as he did when he got excited. "D-D-Don't you want to help us with the uniforms?

Who would know more about uniforms than you, the master of costumes and disguises?"

"Not now," Alex said. "I have important business of my own. And I need to work in Puzzle Club headquarters."

Tobias reached behind the counter and tugged a thick, gold cord. Slowly, one of the display shelves slid to the side. A secret, arched doorway revealed stairs going up to the second floor.

Alex started up the stairs to Puzzle Club headquarters. He reached back and pulled the curtain across the entry to hide it from nosy customers. At the top of the stairs, Alex grabbed the doorknob.

"Don't forget the alarm," Korina called from below.

Alex let go of the doorknob. *That was a close one,* he thought. The Puzzle Club detectives had top-of-the-line security, of course. But if one of the detectives—usually Alex—forgot to punch in the security code, sirens and alarms went off all over the place. It always left Alex totally embarrassed.

He punched in the code. "Of course I didn't forget the alarm," Alex called down to Korina.

Then he walked into Puzzle Club headquarters and slammed the door behind him.

Alex walked past Korina's new invention, something with wires coming out everywhere. He bumped into the examination table, spilling blue liquid from one of Christopher's test tubes. He went straight to his clothes rack. Alex was pretty sure he had the best collection of disguises any detective had ever had.

Alex reached to the top of the rack for his favorite detective hat. His thinking cap, he called it. He lifted the hat. Something flew at him and made him fall backward.

"Sherlock!" Alex cried. He'd wondered where the parakeet, The Puzzle Club's mascot, had been all day. "Keeping cool, boy?" Alex asked, pushing the hat firmly on his head.

"*Braawk! Cool!*" Sherlock squawked.

Sherlock settled onto Alex's shoulder as Alex paced. He and Sherlock had solved many a tough case this way. Alex felt free to think out loud with Sherlock. "What I need," Alex said, "is a perfect way to get even with Patrick Grimaldi. There's no way he's getting a rematch with our team tomorrow."

"*Braawk!*" Sherlock said.

Alex kept pacing. "I could use my ghost disguise and scare him out of town. Or I could disguise myself as an FBI agent. Then I could say Patrick Grimaldi is wanted for spiking somebody in the knee. That's got to be a federal crime."

Alex wasn't sure how much time had passed before he got his best idea. "That's it, Sherlock!" he yelled, scaring the bird back to the clothes rack. "I'll disguise myself as Coach Bryan. All I need are pillows, a uniform ..." Alex grabbed a pillow from his disguise rack.

"Alex! Get down here!" Korina's voice barreled up the stairs and into Puzzle Club headquarters. Alex hated taking orders from Korina. He decided to ignore her.

"Alex! Come here!" Christopher yelled.

Alex couldn't ignore the head of The Puzzle Club. He set down his coach disguise and ran down the stairs. "What's the matter?" Alex asked. "I'm right in the middle of ..."

Alex stopped short. Standing next to Tobias, and looking angry enough to explode, was Sheriff Grimaldi!

"Alex," said the sheriff, stomping across the floor toward him, "I've got some questions to ask you ... about my son. Patrick is missing."

3

Long Gone

Alex felt his throat go dry as he tried to answer Sheriff Grimaldi's questions. How could the sheriff possibly know that Alex had been plotting against Patrick? Alex hadn't talked to anybody. Except Sherlock.

Unless ... Maybe Sheriff Grimaldi had bugged Puzzle Club headquarters. Korina knew how to bug somebody's office so you could hear what they said. The FBI used tape recorders and hidden microphones all the time.

"I-I-I don't know what you heard, Sheriff," Alex began.

Tobias came to the rescue. "Alex, the sheriff is looking for his son Patrick. He's in your class at school, isn't he? I told the sheriff you might know where he's gone."

"I might?" Alex repeated. So maybe Sheriff Grimaldi didn't know about Alex's plan for revenge after all.

Korina chimed in. "And I told the sheriff about the fight you and Patrick almost had after the ball game today."

Leave it to Korina, Alex thought. "So?" he asked weakly.

"Do you have any idea where Patrick went?" asked Sheriff Grimaldi.

"Why would I know where he went?" Alex asked. Then he realized he was sounding too much like a suspect. "I mean, no. I don't know where he went."

"He's probably just playing somewhere," Tobias suggested. "You know boys."

"But I told Patrick I needed him home right after the game. He knew he had to mow the lawn before it got too late. When he didn't come home, I went looking for him. He's nowhere to be found. I don't know where else to look."

The door to Puzzleworks burst open. Joseph Grimaldi stuck his head into the shop. He looked older than 14. Alex knew at least five or six girls who had crushes on Joe Grimaldi.

"Come on, Dad," Joe said. He didn't come inside the store. "You promised we'd work on fly balls. The championship game is tomorrow."

"Hi, Joe," Christopher said. "Come on in."

Joe barely glanced at Christopher before glaring back at the sheriff. "Dad? Are you coming or what?"

Sheriff Grimaldi scratched his head, then turned to his son. "Yeah, I'll be right out, Joe," he said. "Just give me a minute." Joe sighed deeply and left, slamming the front door.

Alex whispered to Korina, "Frankly, I hope Patrick never shows up."

The light fixture above Alex shook from the door slamming. Alex felt something plunk on his head. Then something else. He looked up. Tobias' puzzle lamp shade broke apart and fell into what seemed like a million pieces. It rained plastic giraffes and elephants on Alex's head.

Sheriff Grimaldi didn't even seem to notice as Alex stepped away from the pieces. Christopher and Korina moved in and started picking up the puzzle.

"Alex," said the sheriff, "where exactly was Patrick when you last saw him?"

"On the baseball field," Alex answered quickly.

"Still playing ball?" asked the sheriff. "Even though the game was over?"

"Patrick didn't seem to think the game was over," Korina said. She kept picking up lamp shade puzzle pieces. Alex wished she'd keep her mouth shut. But she went on. "Coach Bryan demanded a rematch. Patrick agreed with him. Coach Miles did not."

"Hmmmm," said Sheriff Grimaldi.

"Yeah," Alex said. "Coach Bryan and Coach Miles were fighting just as much as Patrick and I were—not that we were actually fighting." *Maybe I should keep my mouth shut,* Alex thought.

"The coaches? Did you say Miles? Coach Miles?"

"Yeah," Alex said. "They were screaming at each other. And Patrick was backing Coach Bryan. I think he was telling his coach what to say."

"Hmmmm," Sheriff Grimaldi said again. "I never liked Miles. He was in high school with Coach Bryan and me. I wonder if he knows anything about Patrick's disappearance?"

"I'm sure Coach Miles would let you know if he'd heard anything about Patrick," Christopher said.

"I'm not sure about that," said the sheriff.

The front door flew open again and Joe stepped inside Puzzleworks. Sheriff Grimaldi turned toward the door. "Joe," he said, "I told you I'd be out in a minute."

Joe was staring at something in his hand—an envelope. "Maggie, from your office, gave this to me," he said. "She found it on the steps of the sheriff's office.

Alex ran over to see what it was. So did Korina and Christopher. Joe flipped the envelope over. Funny cutout letters of different sizes spelled out *Sheriff* on the front of the envelope.

Sheriff Grimaldi reached out and took the envelope from Joe's hand. He held it to the light before opening it. Alex saw all color drain from the sheriff's face as he read the letter inside.

"What's it say, Sheriff?" Tobias asked.

The sheriff didn't answer. He looked up, his eyes blank. His hands still held the letter in reading position, as if frozen in place.

"May I look?" Christopher asked.

Sheriff Grimaldi didn't change expressions, but his head moved slightly in a nod.

Christopher took the letter from the sheriff's hands and read:

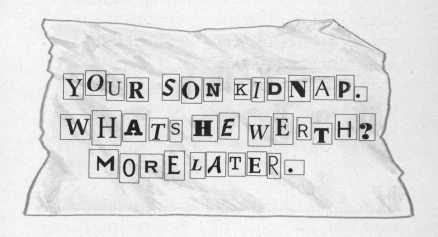

YOUR SON KIDNAP.
WHATS HE WERTH?
MORE LATER.

4

The Kidnapper's Trail

"Kidnapped? Kidnapped?" Sheriff Grimaldi said the words over and over again.

Tobias put his hand on the sheriff's arm. "Sheriff, I'm so sorry. What can we do to help? I'll pray for Patrick. You know God watches over His children. And I'm sure The Puzzle Club will be glad to help in any way they can."

Christopher stepped up. "You can count on The Puzzle Club, Sheriff. We'll get right on the case. We'll find Patrick. Don't you worry. I think we should start ..."

Suddenly the sheriff came to life. "Investigate. I must investigate. My son has been kidnapped! That kidnapper will pay or my name isn't Sheriff Grimaldi!"

"Where do you want us to start?" Korina asked.

Sheriff Grimaldi dismissed her with a wave of his hand. "You kids stay out of my way!" he said. "This is serious police business."

"But couldn't we at least start ..." Christopher began.

"You heard me!" barked the sheriff. "If I find you kids anywhere near this investigation, I'll lock you up myself. That's my son out there. I won't have a bunch of kids playing detective and messing things up!"

Alex started to object, but Christopher shook his head. Alex bit his tongue to keep from saying something.

The sheriff turned his back on The Puzzle Club and headed out the door. "Joe," he said, "we'll have to talk to the coaches first. Then we'll need to organize a search party."

"What about the championship game?" Joe asked.

"There will be no game until we find Patrick!" the sheriff said, slamming the door to Puzzleworks as he left.

Alex turned to Christopher. "Boy, you'd think after all the cases we've solved, Sheriff Grimaldi would be begging us to find Patrick," Alex said. *Like I'd even want to find him,* Alex added to himself.

"He's just upset," Christopher said. "I can't believe Patrick's been kidnapped."

"Well," said Korina, "like it or not, Sheriff Grimaldi *has* let us in on the case." She held up the kidnapper's note. In his rush to leave, the sheriff must have dropped it.

"I'll get my camera," Christopher said. "Let's do what we can." He headed toward the entrance to Puzzle Club headquarters.

"I'll get my magnifying glass and fingerprint powder," Korina said. She followed Christopher to the secret stairway.

"And I'll get my notepad," Alex said.

Once inside Puzzle Club headquarters, the detectives each fell to work. While Christopher snapped pictures of the kidnapper's note, Alex copied the words into his notebook.

Sherlock sat on Alex's shoulder and watched Alex's pencil move. "What's the middle line say?" Alex asked. He tried to get it down before Korina sprinkled her fingerprint powder all over the letters.

Korina answered. "It says, 'What's he worth?' Only the kidnapper misspelled *worth* by putting an *e* instead of an *o*. He certainly isn't very brilliant if he can't even spell correctly," she said.

"So the sheriff can arrest this person for kidnapping *and* misspelling," Alex said. Korina always had to prove how smart she was.

"If misspelling were a crime, then the sheriff could arrest *you,* Alex," Korina said. "So you better be on your best behavior or I'll turn you in myself."

"And by the way," Alex said, "thanks for telling the sheriff I had a fight with Patrick. You …"

"Alex and Korina," Christopher pleaded, "will you two stop arguing? We have more important things going on here. Patrick Grimaldi could be in serious trouble. If we don't figure out where he is and who kidnapped him, we don't know what might happen to him."

Alex felt bad. He still didn't like Patrick, but he didn't want anything bad to happen to him either. *Jesus, I'm sorry about all the mean thoughts I've been having,* Alex prayed silently. *Please keep Patrick safe.*

Korina finished sprinkling the fingerprint powder over the kidnapper's note. She lowered the light over the examination table. Carefully, she tore off a long strip of tape and pressed it to the note. Then she lifted the tape and pressed it onto a white index card. She repeated this until she'd treated the whole note.

Alex tried to peek over Korina's shoulder as she studied her findings through her largest magnifying glass. Sherlock flew from Alex's shoulder to Korina's head.

"Okay," she said. "That does it! Will you two please give me some space?"

"*Braawk! Space!*" Sherlock squawked.

Alex backed away and scribbled all he could remember about the last time he had seen Patrick. Coach Bryan had just threatened Coach Miles with the rematch. Patrick had whispered something into Coach Bryan's ear. He was probably telling his coach the rule about everybody wearing uniforms. Then Coach Bryan and Coach Miles started screaming at each other. The next thing Alex knew, no more Patrick.

"Done," Korina announced.

Christopher, Alex, and Sherlock crowded around Korina's magnifying glass. All the powder had been blown off, leaving those weirdly shaped letters. "What did you find?" Christopher asked.

"I'm afraid not much," Korina said. "I can make out one set of prints, but they're smudged. There's not enough to match, even if the police have the prints on file."

"I've been making enlargements of the photos I took of the note," Christopher said. "If they turn out well, we might be able to match the type of the letters. Then we could find the magazine the kidnapper used to cut out the letters."

Christopher walked back to his developing table and turned on the red lightbulb that hung over his developing tray. "The photos are just starting to come out now. If ..."

But Christopher didn't get a chance to finish his sentence. Tobias yelled up the stairs. "Quick!" he shouted. "Come here!"

Alex, Korina, and Christopher raced down the stairs. Standing next to Tobias was Sheriff Grimaldi. At first Alex was afraid the sheriff would get mad when he saw what Korina had done with the note. But Sheriff Grimaldi was holding another envelope in his hand.

"Did you find Patrick?" Korina asked.

The sheriff hung his head.

Tobias spoke. "There's been no word of Patrick," Tobias said. He glanced at the sheriff, his round eyes full of sadness. "Except for that."

Tobias pointed to the envelope Sheriff Grimaldi clutched in his hands. "The kidnapper has sent another note," Tobias said.

5

The Stakeout

"May I see the note, Sheriff?" Korina asked. She read it out loud.

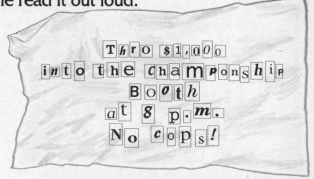

Thro $1,000
into the champonship
Booth
at 8 p.m.
No cops!

Korina said something about spelling, but Alex paid no attention. He was concentrating. Alex knew the booth had to mean the announcer's booth at Victory Field. It was the only field that had an enclosed booth so someone could announce the game. It would be a perfect place for a money drop.

"What are you going to do?" Christopher asked.

"I'll tell you what I'd like to do," the sheriff said. "From what Coach Bryan tells me about the game, my number 1 suspect is Coach Miles. I'd like to go to his house and make him tell me where my son is."

"No way Coach Miles would do this," Alex protested.

"Sheriff, you're wrong," Christopher said calmly. "Coach Miles isn't like that."

"So what do *you* think I should do? My son could be in real danger. I can't stand around here talking all day. If I don't show up with $1,000 by eight o'clock, and that's less than an hour from now, I don't know what will happen to Patrick."

Alex felt sorry for the sheriff. He'd never seen the man look so tired and helpless.

"Do you have the money?" Korina asked.

"All I had in the bank was $323." The sheriff reached into his pocket and pulled out a wrinkled brown bag. He opened it and Alex could see a stack of bills. "I can't call in the state police now. I need your help. I'm sorry about what I said earlier …"

"Don't worry about that," Christopher said. "But where are we going to get the rest of the money?"

Tobias walked behind his counter. He bent

down. A few seconds later he stood up … with a handful of bills. "The good Lord must have known you'd be needing this, Sheriff. I almost never have this much cash at the end of the day. But I sold an order to a restaurant chain today, 37 of those puzzle lamp shades!" He put the money inside Sheriff Grimaldi's paper bag.

"I don't know how to thank you, Tobias," Sheriff Grimaldi said.

"Still," Christopher said, "I don't think that solves all our problems. Sheriff, what do you think about staking out the announcer's booth at Victory Field?"

Alex hadn't even noticed Sherlock on his shoulder. Now the parakeet flapped his wings. "*Braawk! Stakeout!*"

"I don't know," said the sheriff. "The note says no police."

"We won't call in any more police," Christopher explained. "Just you, Korina, Alex, and me. That way we might capture the kidnapper when he tries to pick up the money."

"This is true," said Korina. "Otherwise, what is to prevent the kidnapper from picking up the money and *not* letting Patrick go?"

Korina's words cut Sheriff Grimaldi like a knife. Alex could see him wince at the thought of not getting Patrick back.

"Patrick will be okay," Alex said. "He's a tough kid. I ought to know. Besides, we're praying for him."

"All right," the sheriff said at last. "But if it looks like Patrick is in any danger, we don't move."

The sun was disappearing behind the big oak trees as Korina, Christopher, Alex, and Sherlock made their way to Victory Field. Sherlock perched on Alex's shoulder. He seemed to sense the danger and buried his head in Alex's collar.

Shadows stretched like long fingers across the broken sidewalk. Christopher had explained his plan carefully. The Puzzle Club would surround the announcer's booth. Sheriff Grimaldi would deliver the money as instructed.

The announcer's booth was really just a small, enclosed shack behind home plate. The Puzzle Club couldn't get too close to it without being spotted. The sun had gone all the way down, which meant it was too dark to see inside the booth.

"You two stay behind this tree," Christopher said, leaving Korina and Alex about 20 yards behind the foul line. "Keep Sherlock quiet. I'll try to slip around behind the bleachers. Maybe I can see the kidnapper coming or going."

Christopher left, and Korina and Alex hunched down and waited. Sherlock·covered his eyes with his wings. They didn't have long to wait.

"It's precisely eight o'clock," Korina announced. "Can you see anything, Alex?"

Alex squinted at the dark booth, but he could not make out much. "Listen," he said. "I thought I heard a whine or a cry."

Korina and Alex waited. Then another screech came, louder. Something definitely moved. Alex heard Christopher yell, "Stop!"

"*Braawk! Stop!*" squawked Sherlock.

Korina and Alex charged the booth. It sounded like a fight was going on inside. Alex dived in on top of somebody. Then he felt someone on top of him. They rolled, banging into a chair. Several voices growled or yelled, but Alex could not make out anything.

Sherlock flew wildly, bumping into walls, bodies, furniture. "*Braawk! Fight! Stop!*" the parakeet screeched.

"Wait! Stop!" It was Christopher's voice. And it was coming from underneath Alex. Alex was sitting on top of Christopher!

Alex stood up quickly. Korina slid off his back with a thud. Then a huge figure moaned and got up from the floor.

"Sheriff Grimaldi?" Alex asked.

"Alex? Korina? Christopher?" asked the sheriff. "Then where is the kidnapper?"

"He didn't come," Christopher said. "I saw you jump in and I came to help. I guess you thought I was the kidnapper." Christopher brushed the dust off the sheriff and looked at Alex and Korina. "And you two must have thought we were the kidnappers."

Alex smiled weakly. "Why didn't the real kidnapper show up?"

"I don't know, Alex," Christopher admitted. "It doesn't make any sense. The money's still here." He picked up the brown bag from the floor. Something floated down from it, a scrap of paper.

Korina picked up the paper and pulled a flashlight from her pocket. She shined the light on a ragged scrap of paper. "It's another note," she said. "But this one's written in pencil."

"Why, that's Patrick's handwriting!" said Sheriff Grimaldi. "Let me see that!" He grabbed the note and the flashlight from Korina. "It's from Patrick. He says he's okay."

"Could I please see the note, Sheriff?" Alex asked.

Sheriff Grimaldi handed him the note. In a penciled scrawl, Patrick had written:

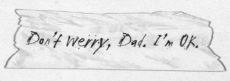

Don't worry, Dad. I'm O.K.

6

Darkness Falls

"Sheriff Grimaldi," Christopher said, "may I hang on to this note?"

The sheriff jerked the note away and held it to his chest. "It's from Patrick," he said. "It's addressed to me."

"I know," Christopher said. "I'll give it back tomorrow. And I won't let anything happen to it."

Sheriff Grimaldi seemed to be studying Christopher in the dark. Slowly he stretched out his arm and let Christopher take the note.

Alex could tell Christopher had something on his mind. But Alex had no idea what it could be. He wanted to ask, but not in front of the sheriff.

Sheriff Grimaldi swung around suddenly and pounded the announcer's table. Alex jumped, bumping into Korina and scaring Sherlock all over again.

"*Now* what do we do?" wailed the sheriff, pounding the table with his fist again. "The kidnapper probably spotted you kids. You didn't hide well enough. I should have known better than to involve children! Now he's taken Patrick, and I may never see him again."

"No one could have seen us, Sheriff," Korina said.

"What do you know about it?" he asked. "I've been wasting hours of precious time. I should have been going after my prime suspect."

"You have a prime suspect?" Alex asked.

"I do!" barked the sheriff. "And if you Puzzle Club kids hadn't talked me out of it, I'd have Coach Miles in custody right now! Who else would want the money delivered to Victory Field?"

"Let's keep our heads, Sheriff," Christopher said. "I'll do a check on the notes and see what I can turn up."

"And as soon as it's light," Korina offered, "I'll come over here and see if I can find any footprints. I'll make plaster casts of them."

40

"You can play detective all you want to," yelled the sheriff. "I'm going to do what I should have done in the first place. I'm going to have a talk with one Coach Miles!" And with that, Sheriff Grimaldi stormed out of the booth and into the darkness.

"Why does he think Coach Miles kidnapped Patrick?" Alex asked. "Do you think it's because I told him the coaches were arguing? I never meant to make Coach Miles a suspect."

"He's just worried about Patrick," Christopher said. "I think we all better get a good night's sleep. In the morning, I'll run an analysis on both notes. Alex and Korina, I need you to collect magazines."

"Magazines?" Alex asked.

"Lots of magazines," Christopher said. "But only recent issues, like from this month."

"What kind of magazines?" Korina asked.

Alex was glad Korina seemed as confused as he was. What could Christopher want with magazines?

"Bring every kind of magazine you can find. Ask your parents. Stop by the library on your way home and tell the librarian how important it is. You should be able to return them tomorrow."

"Uh ... what should we tell the librarian if she asks why we need so many magazines?" Alex asked.

"Tell her the truth. You need them to help solve a mystery. I have a feeling we'd better solve this case fast. Otherwise, Patrick won't be the only one in trouble. Right now, things don't look good for Coach Miles."

The Puzzle Club agreed to meet at 6 A.M. at the headquarters. Then they split up and went their separate ways. Sherlock flew back to Puzzleworks.

As he walked home, Alex thought of all the magazines his mother got. There had to be about a dozen, and that didn't count those his dad got. Korina had told Alex to bring magazines from home. She'd stop by the library since it was on her way home.

As Alex crossed Victory Field, he heard an owl hoot. He could smell somebody's barbecue in the distance. He thought about the way Saturday morning was supposed to have been. He had been headed for the city championship game. He would have played at Victory Field for the first time in his whole life. Now there wouldn't even be a championship game.

As Alex turned onto his own street, he had another thought. What was Patrick Grimaldi thinking tonight? When the case began, Alex hadn't been all that enthused about getting Patrick back. Life without Patrick hadn't seemed that bad. But things had changed, and Alex had to admit he just might be changing too. Tobias had told him that Jesus had a way of changing people's hearts. It had been a long time since he'd thought about getting even with Patrick. Maybe revenge wasn't all it was cracked up to be.

As soon as he got home, Alex darted from room to room, gathering magazines his parents had left lying around. As he climbed into his safe, warm bed that night, Alex still didn't know what good the magazines would do. But he hoped they would work.

Alex turned off the light. His room was totally dark. For a minute, Alex felt scared. What if a kidnapper lurked somewhere in his dark room, waiting to take him just as he'd captured Patrick? Alex prayed. But the first person he prayed for wasn't himself. Alex prayed for Patrick Grimaldi.

7

Letter by Letter

Saturday morning, Alex woke up and shut off his alarm. He dressed faster than he'd ever dressed. Alex grabbed the stack of magazines he'd collected the night before. Then he left a note for his parents and dashed out the door before anybody in his house woke up.

Alex piled as many magazines as he could into his bike basket. The rest he shoved into his backpack. His load was so heavy, he and his bike almost tipped over twice on the ride to Puzzleworks.

The town slept as Alex passed the town square and pulled up beside Puzzleworks. He couldn't believe Korina's bike was already there. How early in the morning did he have to get up to beat her?

Alex remembered to punch in the security

code before he opened the door to Puzzle Club headquarters. The minute he walked inside, Sherlock flew at him and landed on his head. "Morning, Sherlock," Alex said, nearly dropping his stack of magazines.

"Hi, Alex," Christopher called. "Drop the magazines over here by Korina's."

Christopher had fresh photos strung all across the room already. Alex figured his fearless leader must have been there for at least an hour or two. Korina didn't look up from her secret bag of inventions-in-progress. She mumbled something that might have been *hello*. Alex mumbled back.

"What did you find out about the notes?" Alex asked Christopher.

"I have a theory," Christopher said. "But I don't want to say anything until I'm sure. What we need right now is fact. That's where you two—and the magazines—come in. It will help if we can find out where the cutout letters from the first two notes came from. If we know what magazine or magazines were used, we might get a lead."

"And that's why we need all the recent magazines," Korina said. "I had already figured that out on my own."

For the next two hours, Korina and Alex poured over magazines. They examined the style, size, and color of the letters. They tried to find a match on individual letters in the kidnapper's notes. Capital letters showed a greater difference from magazine to magazine, so Alex and Korina focused on those. Tobias brought donuts and milk up to headquarters.

Finally, Korina called out, "I've got it!" She peered through her magnifying glass at the letter *A* in the first note from the kidnapper. Then she moved the magnifying glass to a magazine. "Yes, I knew it!"

Alex and Christopher crowded around for a look. Even Sherlock swooped to the table to examine the letter *A*. Alex saw it. Both letter *A*s were thick on one side, thin on the other, with a special curlicue at the top. And the crossbar on the *A* was lighter than the rest of the letter.

"I agree," Christopher said. "It's a match! See if you find any more matches in that same magazine."

Alex lifted the magazine enough to see the cover. "*Sports Illustrated,*" he said. "I have the newest issue. I'll check it out."

It didn't take long. Alex found identical *W*s, *I*s, *H*s, and *S*s. Between Korina and Alex, nearly two-thirds of the letters used in the kidnapper's notes were found in issues of *Sports Illustrated*.

"I guess this proves the kidnapper read *Sports Illustrated*," Alex said. He was starting to wonder what good their discovery would do for Patrick.

"I'm afraid this won't look good for Coach Miles," Korina said. "Everybody knows he reads *Sports Illustrated* between innings of baseball games."

Suddenly, a noise came from downstairs in Puzzleworks. It was so loud, Alex could clearly hear a man yelling.

"We'd better go down and see what's going on," Christopher said. "Tobias doesn't open the store for another 45 minutes."

Alex was trying to imagine what else could possibly go wrong. Maybe someone had found Patrick! He pushed past Korina to see who was downstairs.

Just inside the door stood Tobias. Sheriff Grimaldi and Coach Bryan were yelling at him. "And if you know where he is and you aren't saying, then you'll have me to answer to," Coach Bryan shouted.

The coach wheeled on Alex as soon as he

saw him. "I wouldn't be a bit surprised if that little one there wasn't in on it," Coach Bryan said, pointing at Alex. "You should have seen the fight he and your boy got into, Sheriff."

Alex opened his mouth, but he didn't know what to say. As if flying to his rescue, Sherlock zoomed at Coach Bryan.

"Get that feathered monster out of my face!" Coach Bryan screamed.

"Have you kids seen Coach Miles?" Sheriff Grimaldi asked, ignoring Sherlock and Coach Bryan.

"Not since yesterday's game," Christopher answered.

"You gonna believe them?" Coach Bryan asked.

Tobias stepped in. "Coach Bryan, if Christopher and The Puzzle Club tell you they haven't see Coach Miles since yesterday, then they haven't seen him since yesterday. You can trust their word."

"Harrumf!" growled Coach Bryan, still trying to swat Sherlock, who was flying in quiet circles around his head.

Sheriff Grimaldi stared at Tobias for a minute. Then he turned back to Christopher. "What about my notes? Did you turn up anything from the kidnapper's notes, anything that will help me find Patrick?"

Alex looked to Christopher. He didn't want to give the sheriff anything he could use against Coach Miles. But evidence was evidence.

"You'd better show Sheriff Grimaldi what we've found so far, Korina," Christopher said.

Nobody said a word while Korina ran upstairs to Puzzle Club headquarters. She returned with the kidnapper's notes and three issues of *Sports Illustrated*.

"After an intense analysis of print media," Korina began, "we traced irrefutable similarities in alphabetical forms."

Alex saw Coach Bryan and Sheriff Grimaldi exchange empty, confused looks.

"The letters match," Alex explained.

Christopher finished the explanation. "Which means the letters the kidnapper used for the notes were cut from issues of *Sports Illustrated*."

"That's it!" said Grimaldi. "That's all we needed." And he and Coach Bryan thundered out of Puzzleworks.

"All they needed for what?" Alex asked.

"To make an arrest, I'm afraid," Christopher said. "I think we just gave them Coach Miles on a silver platter."

8

The Arrest

Sunlight streamed into Tobias' Puzzleworks store, but gloom hung over the room.

"What's that sound?" Korina asked.

Alex listened. "I didn't hear anything," he said.

Then came a plinking, followed by a scratching noise. It was coming from outside. Alex walked over to the window on the far wall of Puzzleworks. He cupped his face in his hands and put his nose to the windowpane to see out.

Suddenly, a face appeared in the window! Alex let out a terrified cry. "Help!" Sherlock flew, beak first at the windowpane, struck it, and fell backward.

"It's Coach Miles," Christopher said.

Christopher opened the window, and Coach Miles climbed inside. He stood before them, his baseball cap in hand. The coach looked as if he hadn't slept all night.

"Coach Miles," Korina said. "What happened to you?"

"Sheriff Grimaldi had me up all night, asking me questions about poor Patrick. Over and over again he asked me about my fight with Coach Bryan and with Patrick. He said people heard me threaten them. The sheriff actually thinks that I kidnapped the boy. Puzzle Club, you have to help me. I don't know where else to turn."

Tobias brought Coach Miles a chair, a glass of milk, and a donut. Coach Miles gobbled down the donut as if he hadn't eaten in a week. "You have to know I didn't have anything to do with this kidnapping," he said.

"Well, of ..." Alex started to say that, of course, The Puzzle Club knew the coach hadn't kidnapped Patrick. But Coach Miles interrupted.

"I wouldn't do anything like that." Coach Miles talked faster and faster. "You have to let me hide out here until you can prove my innocence. Once you solve the case, I'll be safe. But Sheriff Grimaldi and Coach Bryan have never liked me. We went to school together. They were the athletes. I was on the academic team. They've always made fun of me and hated everything I stand for."

Christopher's brow wrinkled. He fiddled with his camera nervously. "Coach," he said, "I just don't know about hiding ..."

"I'd stay out of your way," Coach Miles said, interrupting. "You're my team! I don't have anybody else to trust!"

The words were barely out of his mouth when the Puzzleworks door burst open. In stormed Coach Bryan. Behind him stomped Sheriff Grimaldi.

"We've got him!" Coach Bryan yelled. "Way to go, Puzzle Club!"

Coach Miles looked like a puppy who had just been sent to the dog pound by his loving family. His sad gaze moved from Christopher to Korina to Alex.

Sheriff Grimaldi clamped handcuffs on Coach Miles and pulled him up off his chair. "That last clue you gave us about *Sports Illustrated* was all we needed, kids," he said. "I guess I owe you thanks after all."

"After what you told us, I jogged over to the baseball field," said Coach Bryan. "We found the very magazines he had used to cut out the letters for the ransom notes. They were sitting in his dugout. Four of them had holes on different pages."

"Thanks again, Puzzle Club," said Sheriff Grimaldi. "We'll make him tell us where Patrick is now. I couldn't have made the arrest without you."

Coach Miles looked back at The Puzzle Club as Sheriff Grimaldi dragged him away. "I thought ..." he said. "I thought my own team would believe in me."

9

Footprints in the Sand

Christopher, Korina, Alex, and Tobias stood like statues in Puzzleworks, staring after poor Coach Miles.

"Come on, Puzzle Club," Christopher said, springing into action. "We have work to do."

Alex grabbed his notebook. Christopher threw his camera over his shoulder. Korina reached for her magnifying glass and a sack with her tools and supplies. Then they raced to Victory Field.

The championship baseball field looked different in the morning sunlight. Alex could almost imagine a championship game in play, with him at bat. But as soon as he thought of Patrick at his catcher's position behind the plate, the vision faded.

"What are we looking for ... exactly?" Alex asked.

"Clues," Christopher called from the bleachers.

"Footprints," Korina said. "But don't mess them up if you find them, Alex. I need to make footprint casts." She patted the bag she carried with her.

"I found something!" Christopher hollered from under the bleachers.

Alex and Korina ran to see. Christopher held out a crumpled piece of tinfoil and a long, thin wrapper.

Alex took a closer look at the paper wrapper. "It's cinnamon gum!" he said. "That's the kind Patrick always chews."

"Keep looking," Christopher said.

While Korina and Christopher started at each entrance to the field, Alex walked back to the announcer's booth. The first thing he noticed was a clump of sand just outside the booth. Alex scribbled his observation in his notebook. He saw a few more grains of the coarse, brown sand inside the booth.

When he didn't find any more sand, Alex looked outside again. Sand lay in a scattered trail from the booth across the entry walk. Alex picked up the trail.

"What did you find, Alex?" Korina asked. She had crept up behind him without Alex noticing. "Step aside," she said, trying to edge in front of him.

"It's my discovery, Korina," Alex said. He held his ground.

"But I'm the footprint expert," Korina said.

Christopher stood in front of them, his hands on his hips. "Korina, Alex, stop it."

Korina and Alex let their leader take the lead. Christopher followed the sand across the short walk. "It leads through the sandlot," he said. The baseball field was flanked by sandlots. It cut down on the mud tracked onto the bleachers during the rainy season.

"What a break!" Korina said, getting out her tools and materials. "I should be able to make perfect casts of the footprints."

Christopher and Alex bent over the trail of footprints, one on either side. Alex could clearly make out three different prints. One print had holes in it. It might have been made by a tennis shoe, a much bigger size than Alex wore. A second print was bigger yet. Alex had no idea what kind of shoe would have made it. The third print was the oddest. Alex could see a deep heel mark. In front of it, the sole print stretched long to a point at the front. The heel was too big and the sole too long to belong to a woman's high-heel shoe.

Christopher snapped photos from every angle. He stood right over each print and took shots. He knelt close to the sand and clicked frontways and sideways and upside down.

Meanwhile, Korina poured a brown powder into a metal bowl. She squirted in something from a plastic bottle. "Alex," she called, "find me a strong stick."

Alex found one, though he thought Korina should have said *please.* "How's this?" he asked, handing her the thickest stick he could find.

"I guess it will have to do," Korina said. She stirred her mixture with both hands. The bowl wobbled, so Alex held it while she stirred.

After a few minutes of stirring, the brown liquid got as thick as oatmeal. "I'm almost ready," Korina called to Christopher. "Are you finished with the pictures?"

Christopher snapped two more shots. "Okay," he said. "Pour."

Korina filled three different prints with her mixture—one for each kind of shoe Alex had spotted. She took extra time with the tennis shoe print, being careful to get each little circle of the sole imprint.

"That one's the tennis shoe of a big man," Alex said.

"You're jumping to conclusions again, Alex," Korina said. "I'll have facts once these molds harden."

"Well," Alex said, "at least we know now there were three kidnappers."

Korina sighed deeply. Alex knew she wanted to accuse him of jumping to conclusions again. She was always so slow to figure these things out. It would be up to him to guess who the three kidnappers were. If they waited on Korina's "facts," Patrick might never be found.

It took awhile for Korina's plaster to set enough to remove. Then they each carried one mold and returned to headquarters.

Christopher set to work developing his pictures. Korina started examining the molds through her magnifying glass. She sprayed something on each one and stared at them again.

Alex couldn't stand the wait. He was trying to guess who the three men might have been. Escaped prisoners? Ghosts of long-gone championship baseball stars?

Sherlock kept interrupting Alex's thoughts. The crazy parakeet flapped his wings in Alex's face. Then it flew at Alex's stomach. Finally, Sherlock flew away, then returned with a piece of donut in his beak, which he dropped in Alex's hair.

"Hey, Sherlock!" Alex scolded. Then he realized Sherlock was trying to tell him something. "I get it. You're starving." Alex had forgotten to feed him in all the hassle of the morning.

"Sorry, Sherlock," Alex said, setting out the parakeet food The Puzzle Club kept for their mascot. Alex thought about Patrick. He hoped the prison escapees were feeding him.

"Running shoe, army boot, and cowboy boot," Korina announced. She lay down her magnifying glass, obviously certain of her conclusions.

Alex dropped the birdseed on the floor. Running shoe, army boot—those could belong to anybody. But the cowboy boot? There was only *one* person in town who wore cowboy boots. "Sheriff Grimaldi?" Alex asked, his voice cracking. "Sheriff Grimaldi kidnapped his own son?"

10

Mystery to Boot

"Alex," Christopher said, "you can't go around accusing the sheriff of kidnapping his own son. Why would he do a thing like that?"

"Sheriff Grimaldi *is* the only one we know who wears cowboy boots," Korina said.

"So I'm not jumping to conclusions," Alex said, glad Korina was on his side for once.

"I still think something's wrong here," Christopher said.

"Well," Korina said, sounding hurt that Christopher would question her scientific results, "shouldn't we at least check it out?"

Christopher sighed. "Okay," he said. "We'll talk to the sheriff. But let me do the talking, okay? I don't want you two calling him a kidnapper."

Sheriff Grimaldi's office was on the other side of the town square. When The Puzzle Club got there, the sheriff was pacing the sidewalk outside his office. He stared in one direction, then in the other. Coach Bryan stood guarding the door.

"So it's you," Coach Bryan said. "You can't talk to the prisoner. Your Coach Miles still hasn't told us where Patrick is."

"We haven't come to talk to Coach Miles," Christopher said. He tried to go in, but Coach Bryan blocked the doorway.

"Let 'em in," Sheriff Grimaldi said, shoving in front of everyone. He plopped in the chair behind his desk.

Coach Bryan kept his arm on the doorpost. Christopher, Alex, and Korina ducked and filed in under the man's huge, bulging biceps.

"What is it?" asked the sheriff. "Do you have any more clues on what Coach Miles might have done with my boy?"

Alex couldn't stand thinking of Coach Miles in the other room, behind bars. "We know for sure Coach Miles didn't do it!" Alex blurted out.

Sheriff Grimaldi shoved his chair backward and charged from behind his desk. "What do you mean?" he roared.

Alex's knees felt like Jello. "We ... we ... you ... shoes ..." he stammered.

"Pssst, Alex!" Korina whispered. "Look!" She pointed to Sheriff Grimaldi's feet.

Alex looked. He stopped in mid-sentence when he saw what Korina was pointing to. Sheriff Grimaldi was wearing black patent leather shoes!

"But ... but your boots?" Alex asked. "Your cowboy boots?"

"What?" Sheriff Grimaldi asked, looking totally confused. He looked down at his feet. "I hate these blamed shoes. They're my Sunday-go-to-meetin' shoes."

"Where *are* your cowboy boots, Sheriff?" Christopher asked.

"That's what I'd like to know," said the sheriff. "I haven't seen them since I loaned them to Joe last Wednesday. These things are killing my feet." He rubbed his toes. "But what's that got to do with the price of beans?"

"When we find out," Christopher said, "you'll be the first to know." Christopher darted out of the sheriff's office. Korina and Alex ran to catch up.

"Where are we going now?" Alex asked, trying to keep up.

"Unless I miss my guess," Korina said, "we're on our way to pay a visit to one Joseph Grimaldi."

"Did you say *guess*, Korina?" Alex asked. "Detective work is not guesswork." Korina frowned at Alex and ran faster.

Alex was the last one to reach the Grimaldi home. Korina and Christopher were already standing on the steps of the front porch. Joseph Grimaldi sat on the porch swing, tossing his baseball up into the air and catching it in his mitt.

"We would have killed you!" Joe told Christopher.

Alex gasped. He was ready to turn around and run the other way until he realized Joe was just talking about the championship game.

"Maybe," Christopher said, good-natured as always.

"This was my last chance in this league," Joe said. "I worked hard for this game. Patrick never works hard at anything."

"Actually," Korina said, "we've come about Patrick."

"Figures," Joe said. "He turn up yet?"

"No," Christopher said quickly. "We wanted to ask you about your father's cowboy boots."

"Those things?" Joe asked. "I wouldn't be caught dead in cowboy boots. Talk about uncool."

"Your dad said you borrowed them last Wednesday," Alex said.

Joe looked like he was trying to remember back that far. "Oh that," he said. "Ants. I got ants in my bedroom. I just needed something to stomp them out. I took Dad's boots. So what?"

"Probably nothing, really," Christopher said. "Do you think we could take a look at the boots?"

Joe looked as if Christopher had asked him to do a thousand push-ups. But he got to his feet. "I guess. But it seems stupid to me."

He walked into the house, leaving The Puzzle Club on the porch. It seemed to Alex that Joe was inside for a long time. Finally he came out, holding one cowboy boot. "That's weird," Joe said. "I looked all over my room, but I can't find the other cowboy boot."

"He's got the left boot," Korina said. "The footprint was made by the right boot."

"He's hiding the evidence!" Alex said. "Where's Patrick? What have you done with your brother?"

"Are you crazy or something?" Joe asked.

"Calm down, Alex," Christopher said. "Something's still not right about all this."

"But look at the facts, Christopher," Korina said. She sounded defensive again, like she thought Christopher didn't trust her analysis. "I got good, clean prints of each type of shoe. One print of each."

"That's it!" Christopher said. "I knew something wasn't right. *One* print of each!"

11

The Pieces Fit Together

Christopher jumped off the porch and raced down the driveway away from the Grimaldi's house. Joe stood open-mouthed, one cowboy boot in his hand.

There was nothing left for Korina and Alex to do but chase after Christopher. They didn't catch up with him until they reached Puzzleworks. Christopher was already inside headquarters, studying his photographs.

"Look at these," he said, pointing to a set of photos lined up on the clothesline. "Where are the matching prints? All the cowboy boot prints are of a right cowboy boot. The army boot is a left shoe in every picture. See what I mean? One person made all these prints."

It was clear as day once Christopher pointed it out.

Christopher took out pictures of the three notes. "This is what was troubling me the whole time. It's what made me form my theory yesterday. Look at the first note from the kidnapper and the note Patrick wrote in pencil. What do you notice that's the same?" Korina and Alex studied the photographs of the two notes side by side.

"Nothing's the same," Alex said. "One's in cutout letters. One's in pencil. I don't get it."

But Korina looked like a lightbulb had clicked on in her brain. "Both were written by poor spellers!" she said.

"Right," Christopher said. "But even more. *Worth* in the first note should be spelled with an *o* instead of an *e*. Patrick made the exact same mistake in *his* note."

Korina held the notes to the light. "*Werry!*" she said. "Patrick used an *e* instead of an *o*."

Slowly, the answer was dawning on Alex. One boot. One tennis shoe. One cowboy boot. And the spelling. "Patrick always has been an even worse speller than I am," Alex said. "We're usually the first two to sit down in spelling bees."

"What do we do now?" Korina asked.

Christopher picked up his baseball and glove instead of his camera. "I think it's about time for The Puzzle Club to play in a championship game after all. Come on."

Christopher walked to the big painted eye at the far side of the room. When he touched it, a circle opened and revealed the secret exit from Puzzle Club headquarters. He climbed to the top of the chute. "Puzzle Club!" he hollered. "To Victory Field!" And he disappeared down the chute, clunking as he went.

"To Victory Field!" Alex shouted, beating Korina to the secret chute. He smiled back at her with his most winning grin. "Detectives first!"

Once at Victory Field, Christopher motioned for Korina to take her place on the pitcher's mound. Alex moved close to the third base dugout, and Christopher stood at home plate.

Alex took a step. Something crackled underneath his foot. He bent down to pick it up. It was a wrapper from a stick of cinnamon gum. Alex knew they were on the right track. He edged closer to the dugout. Then he waved the wrapper at Christopher and Korina so they could see it too.

Christopher tossed the ball to Korina. She threw it harder to Alex. Alex wasn't sure what their leader had in mind, but he was willing to play along. He threw the ball toward home plate.

"Yeah," Christopher said, throwing again to Korina, "it's a shame we won't have a championship game this year."

"Sure is," Korina added.

"I think so too," Alex said, not knowing what else to say.

Christopher took over again. "Who would have thought poor Sheriff Grimaldi would go to pieces like this? I've never seen anything like it."

Alex thought he heard something move inside the dugout. It was all he could do not to turn and look. But he was starting to get the picture. "Yeah," he said, "the sheriff looked so old and worn out. He didn't sleep a wink all night."

"That's for sure!" Korina said, a note of anger in her voice. "How could he? He was grilling poor, innocent Coach Miles all night long. Coach Miles, who never hurt anyone in his life! Now, he's been accused unfairly ..."

Christopher cut Korina off with a look. Even Alex knew Korina wasn't getting across the message Christopher had in mind. Since he was closest to the dugout, it was up to him.

"Sometimes," Alex said, trying to find the right words, "the way dads yell at you—and sometimes the way they *don't*—it's hard to believe how much they really love you."

"That's right, Alex," Christopher said.

Korina must have finally gotten the point. She didn't want to be left out. She whizzed the ball to Alex so hard, he dropped it. "Like Sheriff Grimaldi," Korina said. "I never would have taken him for the emotional type. But every time I see him, he's got tears in his eyes. He really misses Patrick."

"You know," Alex said. "I'll bet Sheriff Grimaldi would give anything to have Patrick home again."

Christopher surprised Alex. "Nah," he said. "Don't you think he'll be really mad at Patrick for running away?"

Alex gave Christopher a shocked look. What did Christopher think he was doing now?

Christopher winked at him and nodded toward the dugout.

"Oh, I get it," Alex said. "I mean, you're wrong, Christopher. Of course, the sheriff would be glad to have his son home. He loves Patrick so much, he'd forgive him for anything! He'd be that happy to have him back. That's all he can think about."

"That's the truth," said Korina. "I see him looking out the window of his office. He walks out and looks down the street, like he's watching for Patrick to come home."

Korina whipped the ball at Alex. He caught it, but it stung his hand. Alex threw the ball back at her as hard as he could. She caught it easily. "It reminds me of that story Tobias told us," Korina said. "The one from the Bible. The one about the prodigal son. You know the one I mean, Christopher?"

"Yeah," Alex said. "I'd like to hear that one too, Christopher. How'd it go? Come on up here closer. I can hardly hear you when you're standing by home plate."

Christopher and Korina joined Alex. They sat down in the grass, their backs to the dugout. Alex wanted to peek inside so badly, he could almost taste it. What if they were going through all of this for nothing? But he had the gum wrapper in his pocket, so he felt pretty sure they were on the right track.

"Now, I can't tell it as well as Tobias does," Christopher said, "but it goes kind of like this. A father had two sons. The younger son asked his dad for the money that would be his when his dad died. Then he ran away to have some fun. But soon he ran out of money."

"I remember now," Korina said. "The son did not have any place to sleep at night. But the worst thing of all was how much he missed his dad. Pretty soon he started feeling horrible. He thought, 'Even deputies—I mean, servants—do better than this. They don't have to sleep on cold, hard benches ...' "

Christopher stopped her. "That's it. So even though the son was afraid his father might be mad at him, he decided it was worth the risk. He wanted to come home. He started walking home. On the way he thought about what he'd say to his dad. He decided to say, 'I'm sorry, Father, for making you worry. I don't deserve to be your son. Just let me live like a servant and work for you, and that will be good enough.' "

Christopher stopped talking. Alex could almost feel someone peeking out from the dugout. So Alex asked the question he figured that someone was thinking. "And what did the father do?"

Christopher smiled. "Why, it turns out the father had been waiting and waiting for his son to come home. When the son was still a little ways off, his father saw him. He ran to his son and threw his arms around him. The son apologized and said everything he'd planned to say. But the father forgave him and welcomed him back as a son. And besides that, he threw a huge party because he was so happy his son had come back to him."

Alex heard footsteps tiptoe out of the dugout. He turned around and so did Korina and Christopher. There stood Patrick Grimaldi.

12

A Home Run

"Did that dad really forgive the kid?" Patrick asked. He still had on his baseball uniform, but it was torn and wrinkled. His baseball cap looked crushed, and his hair stuck out.

"He really did," Christopher said.

"I didn't want to make him so worried," Patrick said. "I just wanted him ... to notice."

"I know," Christopher said, "because he spends so much time getting Joe ready to play baseball and goes to *his* games instead of to yours."

Patrick looked at the ground, but he nodded.

"I'm sure your dad didn't know it meant so much to you, Patrick," Christopher said. "Your dad loves you just as much as he loves Joe."

"I know ... now," Patrick said. "I'm really sorry for all this."

The Puzzle Club walked with Patrick back into town. After they'd walked a few yards in silence, Patrick asked, "I don't get why you guys bothered finding me. Especially you, Alex."

Alex tried to put it into words. "I guess it's something God did inside me," he said. "To tell the truth, when you disappeared, I can't say I felt sorry."

"Alex!" Korina scolded.

"No," Patrick said. "Alex and I have never been friends. I want to hear what happened. Go on, Alex."

"At first," Alex said, "I thought I wanted to get even with you for spiking me at home plate. But after a while, I started worrying about you. All that other stuff didn't seem so important. I'm sorry about the mean things I said. Forgive me?"

"Yeah," Patrick said. "I was pretty rotten to you too."

"Sounds like you both learned a little about forgiveness," Christopher said.

Patrick gave Alex a pat on the back. "Thanks, Alex," he said. Then Patrick explained how he'd taken the three different shoes to make everybody think there were three kidnappers. He'd been hiding out in the dugout most of the time. And he'd had a lot of time to think.

"Is that story you guys told really true?" Patrick asked. "Is it really in the Bible?"

"Jesus told the story Himself," Christopher said. "He told it so we'd know how much God loves us, that God loves us like a father and forgives us no matter how much we mess up."

Patrick seemed to be thinking about that one. He didn't speak again until they were almost to town.

They had just turned onto the town square when Alex spotted Sheriff Grimaldi. The sheriff held his hand against his forehead, as in a salute, shielding his eyes from the sun as he looked up and down the street. His gaze came to rest on The Puzzle Club and Patrick. Sheriff Grimaldi took off in a run straight toward them.

At first, Alex was scared to see the sheriff charging. Then he got a look at Sheriff Grimaldi's face and the tears streaming down his cheeks. His arms stretched wide as he reached Patrick. Then he grabbed his son off the ground and swung him in a circle. Tobias came running up and joined in the congratulations.

"We found him hiding out in the dugout, Tobias," Christopher explained while Sheriff Grimaldi listened. "There never was any kidnapper. Patrick did it all himself."

"I'm sorry, Dad. I'm so sorry. I didn't mean to worry you," Patrick said. "I never should have run away. I just …"

Christopher nudged him. "Go on, Patrick."

"I just wanted you to pay attention to me, Dad," Patrick said. "Will you forgive me?"

His father hugged him again. "Of course, I forgive you, son. I'm sorry too. I haven't given you enough attention. I've been all caught up in my job and Joe's baseball career. Things are going to be better around here. You'll see."

Sheriff Grimaldi hugged Patrick so long and so hard, Alex was afraid Patrick's eyes might pop out. They were laughing and crying at the same time.

"Welcome home, Patrick!" shouted Coach Miles from the jail window.

Sheriff Grimaldi tossed his keys to Christopher, who ran to free his coach. "I owe you an apology, Miles," the sheriff yelled.

As Alex watched Patrick and his dad, a strange warmth spread through him. If he didn't look out, Alex might start crying along with them.

Korina elbowed Alex. "Hey, I thought you didn't care if Patrick ever came back," she said, grinning.

Alex grinned. "I'm just as surprised as you are," he said. "Guess we were both wrong." Alex *was* glad Patrick was home. He might even try harder to get to know him.

"One more thing, Dad," Patrick said. "The Puzzle Club said something about a party you were throwing. Something about celebrating that I'm home again?"

Sherlock swooped down and landed on Alex's shoulder. "*Braawk! Party! Party!*"

"We were just telling him the story of the prodigal son, Tobias," Alex explained. "You know, that part in the end where the father is so glad to have his son back that he kills a fat calf and throws a feast?"

"A *fatted* calf, Alex," Korina corrected. "Not a *fat* calf."

Patrick laughed. Then everybody joined in. Except Alex. He had just remembered the very end of the prodigal son story. In it, the older brother was so jealous and angry, he refused to come to the party for his brother. Alex hoped Joe wouldn't be like that.

Somebody nudged Alex aside and walked past. Joe stood beside his father. He looked at Patrick. Then he grinned and patted him on the back. "Welcome back, brother," he said.

That night the town held the championship baseball picnic as planned. Coach Miles and Coach Bryan were there, acting like buddies for the first time in their lives. Coach Miles said he forgave everybody and was just glad Patrick was safe. Alex watched with Christopher and Korina as Sheriff Grimaldi played catch with both his sons.

Tobias put a hand on Alex's shoulder. "So it's a happy ending all around, eh?" he asked.

"Not bad," Alex said. "Now will somebody please show me to the fat calf? I'm starving!"